DATE DUE

Call Me Aram

For Elizabeth Clancy,
who loves books
M. S.

Thank you, Alexander and the Gang
M. W.

NEW BEGINNINGS

Call Me Aram

By Marsha Forchuk Skrypuch

with illustrations by Muriel Wood

Fitzhenry & Whiteside

Text copyright © 2009 by Marsha Forchuk Skrypuch
Illustration copyright © 2009 by Muriel Wood

Published in Canada by Fitzhenry & Whiteside,
195 Allstate Parkway, Markham, Ontario L3R 4T8

Published in the United States by Fitzhenry & Whiteside,
311 Washington Street, Brighton, Massachusetts 02135

10 9 8 7 6 5 4 3 2 1

Library and Archives Canada Cataloguing in Publication
Skrypuch, Marsha Forchuk, 1954-
Call me Aram / Marsha Forchuk Skrypuch ; illustrated by Muriel Wood.
ISBN 978-1-55455-000-5 (bound).--ISBN 978-1-55455-001-2 (pbk.)

1. Armenian massacres, 1915-1923--Turkey--Juvenile fiction.
2. Orphans--Juvenile fiction. I. Wood, Muriel II. Title.
PS8587.K79C35 2008   jC813'.54   C2008-902321-8

U.S. Publisher Cataloging-in-Publication Data
(Library of Congress Standards)

Skrypuch, Marsha Forchuk, 1954-
Call me Aram / Marsha Forchuk Skrypuch ; illustrated by Muriel Wood.
[86] p. : col. ill., map ; cm.
Includes index.

Summary: A group of refugee orphans escape the Armenian genocide in Turkey and are sent to a farm in Georgetown, Ontario, where they must adjust to the unfamiliar habits and customs of their Canadian sponsors.
ISBN-13: 978-1-55455-000-5
ISBN-13: 978-1-55455-001-2 (pbk.)
1. Armenian massacres survivors – Ontario -- Juvenile fiction. 2. Georgetown (Ont.) --
Juvenile fiction. I. Wood, Muriel. II. Title.
[Fic] dc22   PZ7.S5797Ca 2008

Fitzhenry & Whiteside acknowledges with thanks the Canada Council for the Arts, and the Ontario Arts Council for their support of our publishing program. We acknowledge the financial support of the Government of Canada through the Book Publishing Industry Development Program (BPIDP) for our publishing activities.

Canada Council for the Arts   Conseil des Arts du Canada   ONTARIO ARTS COUNCIL   CONSEIL DES ARTS DE L'ONTARIO

Design by Wycliffe Smith

Printed in Hong Kong

Table of Contents

July 2, 1923

Georgetown Boys' Farm

As Aram slept, images flitted through his mind. Escaping the war in Turkey with his grandmother. Playing marbles with the other boys at the orphanage in Corfu. Leaning over the railing of the boat. Waving the golden veil his grandmother had given him.

Waving good-bye.

Leaving her behind.

Then Aram dreamt that his grandmother was bending over him as he slept. His cheek tickled as she brushed it with her fingertips.

"You are safe now, and so am I," she said.

Aram snuggled deeper into his dream.

"Wake up, lazybones!"

The image of his grandmother evaporated. His cheek tickled again. Aram shielded his eyes from the sun overhead. He squinted.

Mikayel was standing over him. Aram remembered where he was—on a grassy hill at Georgetown Boys' Farm in Canada. And he was safe.

Mikayel dangled something against Aram's cheek, and he felt the tickle again. Through squinting eyes, he saw wiggling hairs. It was a funny-looking spider with amazing long legs. Aram knocked Mikayel's hand away and sat up.

"What did you do that for?" asked Aram with annoyance, rubbing the dreams out of his eyes.

"You wouldn't wake up," said Mikayel. "Come on!" Then he ran down the hill.

Was it just three weeks since his grandmother had waved good-bye to him at the dock in Corfu? So much had happened since then. He and forty-five other boys had traveled halfway around the world, by boat, train, and ship. He was in Canada now, far away from war. And the missionary back in Corfu had promised to look after his grandmother.

Aram stood up and brushed the wrinkles out of his shorts. His blanket was damp with dew, so he shook it out before folding it. All the other blankets were gone.

So were the other boys. He looked down at the valley and grinned in appreciation.

The farm seemed as wide as the ocean. To his left a creek wound through the valley, and fruit and willow trees grew everywhere. Directly below he could see the new dormitory and a red-bricked farmhouse. Aram was used to being in cramped quarters—on the streets in Ankara, Turkey, begging with his grandmother after his parents had been killed, or at the orphanage on the Greek island of Corfu with thousands of other children. He stretched his arms wide and breathed in the morning air.

Then he threw his blanket over his shoulder and walked down the hill.

When he passed the long stucco dormitory at the bottom of the hill, Aram got a whiff of drying plaster. As soon as the building was finished, he and the other boys would sleep in there instead of on the hill, under the stars. He longed to go inside the new building and explore. Would it look the same as their barracks in Corfu?

Rows of picnic tables had been set up in front of the farmhouse. Aram took his seat beside Mikayel. The other boys were already sitting there, spoons in hand and stomachs grumbling. He looked down the rows of familiar faces and felt a twinge of sadness. Mgerdich wasn't here. He had fallen from the train and now was in a hospital in France. Aram wondered if the ragged cut on his little friend's face had healed. Would the hospital release him soon? Three other boys had also been held back for health reasons. At least Mgerdich wasn't alone.

A pitcher of milk and a bowl of sugar sat on each picnic table. Aram was so hungry that he felt like grabbing a spoonful of the golden sugar, but he knew that would be rude.

The door of the farmhouse opened and Reverend Edwards stepped out. He carried a huge steaming pot. Grunting from the weight of it, he set it in the middle of one of the picnic tables, and then he smiled. Mrs. Edwards followed with a tray stacked with bowls.

She set the tray down beside the pot. Pointing to Zaven, she motioned for him to step forward. Zaven scrambled out of his seat, an anxious look in his eyes. The reverend's wife handed him a bowl and motioned for him to hold it up in front of the reverend.

Reverend Edwards swirled a huge ladle in the pot and drew it out. It was filled with something steamy, gluey, and gray. He glopped it into Zaven's bowl and grinned. All the boys watched nervously as they waited for their friend to sniff it. Zaven wrinkled his nose in disgust. The boys groaned.

"Mmmmm!" said Mrs. Edwards, rubbing her stomach and pointing at the glop. "Oatmeal porridge."

None of the boys spoke English, and Aram had no idea what *oatmeal porridge* meant. He knew it was something to eat in the morning. It looked as if Mrs. Edwards thought it was tasty. How he wished that the reverend and his wife spoke Armenian!

She motioned for the next boy to approach, and then the next. Each boy went up to the front, and each said, "Thank you," which was one of the few phrases they had learned in English. When it was Aram's turn, he thanked Mrs. Edwards as she served him the steamy mess. He carried it back to his place. He sat down and stared into the bowl. It looked even worse up close. Aram had eaten orange peels and apple cores. He had even eaten food out of garbage heaps, but he had never eaten goo—and lumpy gray goo at that! The smell reminded him of dirt after rain.

Aram looked around. All the boys were staring into their bowls, but no one had dipped in their spoons. Then Reverend Edwards served big bowls of the goo for himself and his wife. Aram watched as they sprinkled the glop with sugar and poured some milk onto it.

"Good porridge!" exclaimed Reverend Edwards.

Aram's stomach grumbled. He sprinkled his porridge with a bit of sugar and poured some milk over it, too. As he dipped his spoon into the porridge, he looked up. All eyes were on him. He put the spoon into his mouth.

Horrible! Porridge tasted as bad as it looked. Aram was about to crumple his face in disgust when he caught a glimpse of the reverend and his wife. They looked so anxious to please. He didn't want to hurt their feelings, so he swallowed it.

"How is it?" asked Mikayel.

"I haven't decided," said Aram, taking another spoonful. He didn't want to lie, but he didn't want to be the only one eating this stuff either.

Mikayel dipped his spoon into his porridge and tasted it.

"Ugh!" He shoved the bowl away and crossed his arms. Other boys also tried a bit of the porridge. No one liked it except for Zaven, who dug in hungrily, unaware of the questioning stares.

CHAPTER 2

Exploring

After breakfast the boys gathered their bowls and spoons, and wiped the tables clean. Mrs. Edwards motioned with her hands that they could explore the grounds if they wanted to. Aram, Mikayel, and a few other older boys stayed behind to wash the dishes. Once they were finished, Mrs. Edwards smiled and nodded her thanks.

"You go play now, too," she said slowly in a loud voice.

Aram nodded back. He was fairly certain he understood what she was trying to say to them. The two boys walked past the dormitory building. They paused for a moment to watch a couple of workers wheel in a huge wooden crate.

"Let's see what's in it," said Mikayel.

The boys walked alongside the building and around the corner. They stood on tiptoe and looked in through the first window  they came to. The crate wasn't there. The room was longer than it was wide. Against one wall was a row of single beds. Against the opposite wall was a row of bunk beds. The mattresses were bare.

"This must be our new bedroom," said Aram. "It looks finished to me."

They walked around to the other side of the building and peered in through a set of windows directly opposite the front door.

"There's the box," said Aram.

From where they stood, Aram and Mikayel could see the men push the bulky wooden crate through the door-way. In the room stood a tall wooden cabinet with hinged doors on its front.

"This is a Canadian-style kitchen," said Mikayel.

"How can you tell?"

"That's an icebox," said Mikayel, pointing to the cabinet. "Don't you remember? There was a giant one in the ship's galley."

Aram stood on his tiptoes and took a second look at the cabinet. "I think you're right."

He had never seen such a thing in his life until their trip across the ocean. On the *S.S. Minnedosa*, a woman who worked there spoke Armenian. She had taken the boys to the ship's kitchen and had opened the icebox to show them how it worked. In one of the compartments stood a big block of ice, which had to be replaced every few days. The ice kept the food cold, so it would last longer without spoiling.

Aram had been very young when his mother was killed, but he could still remember her twice-daily trip to the market for fresh food. His home town of Ulus, in Ankara, would get scorching hot in the summer. Meat could be full of maggots in a matter of hours. His mother would have loved an icebox. A tear formed in the corner of Aram's eye, but he brushed it away quickly before Mikayel saw.

The men pried the front off the wooden box.

"Wow," said Aram. "It's a stove like the one we saw on the ship!"

Stews had been cooked over an open fire at the orphanage in Corfu, but most everything else was eaten raw. Back in Ulus his mother would simmer wheat-berry pilaf for hours in the *ojak*, the cooking hearth inside their house. Each week she and the neighborhood women would gather at a common hearth, in the courtyard at the end of the street. There they would bake *lahvosh*, the broad, thin cracker bread that they would eat every day.

This Canadian oven looked nothing like a hearth or an *ojak*. It was a huge, shiny metal monster that looked more like part of a train than something to cook with. Maybe that was why Canadians couldn't make tasty foods like pilaf or *lahvosh*. These big monster ovens could only cook strange foods like porridge and spongy white bread.

Then Aram heard the familiar screeching sound of the radial railway's brakes.

"There must be someone getting off at the stop," he said to Mikayel. "Come on!"

The two boys ran down the path that led to the railway stop. Aram's heart pounded. Would Mgerdich arrive? Ever since Mgerdich had fallen out of the train window, he had been on Aram's mind. Mgerdich was more like a brother than a friend.

People appeared on the path. Aram's heart sank—no Mgerdich. It was more Canadians. These ones were dressed in similar clothing to those who had given them Canadian flags and greeted them at the farm the day before. But Aram wasn't sure if they were the same people. Canadians all looked alike—the men wore dark suits and shiny shoes, and the women wore light colored dresses, with hats over their curly hair.

Aram and Mikayel followed the strangers back to the grounds and joined the other boys. One woman, whose hat was bigger than the rest, stepped forward and smiled kindly. She reached into her handbag and drew out a dozen or so brightly colored pebble-like objects. They made a crinkly sound in the palm of her hand.

"Candy," she said loudly. "Have one." And she reached her hand out to Aram.

Why did Canadians talk so loudly to them? Aram wondered. They didn't speak so loudly to each other. Aram didn't know what *candy* was, so he took a tiny step forward and gazed into her hand.

"Mmmm," said the woman, just as Mrs. Edwards had when she introduced them to the porridge.

If those pebbly things tasted like porridge, Aram didn't want one. He shook his head and stepped back. The woman kneeled down. She placed all of the *candy* in her lap, took one, and tugged on both ends of the crinkly wrapper. The wrapper slid off, and a pale stone popped out.

"Butterscotch candy," she said, then handed the unwrapped object to Aram.

The reverend's wife walked over to where the guests had gathered.

"Welcome!" she said. Then she looked down at Aram and smiled as he considered the object in his hand.

"You will like it," she said, nodding encouragingly.

Aram sniffed the candy; it didn't smell like porridge. He placed it on his tongue, and a sugary-buttery taste exploded in his mouth.

"Thank you!" he said, grinning.

The woman looked pleased as the other boys gathered around her and sampled this delicious Canadian food called *butterscotch candy*.

CHAPTER 3

Click! Flash!

O ne of the Canadian men held a strange wooden box up to his face and pointed it in the direction of the boys.

"Smile!" he said.

"Duck!" cried Aram in Armenian. The boys dropped their candies and fell to the ground. Like all Armenian children, Aram had learned to avoid strange objects that were pointed at him. Too many strange objects turned out to be weapons.

The man gasped at their reaction.

"No," he said. "It's fine. It is a camera. Look." The man knelt down beside Aram and held the object out to him.

Aram lifted his head and looked over to the reverend's wife. She did not seem to be alarmed by the object. She nodded and motioned with her hands for Aram and the rest of the boys to stand up.

Again, Aram wished he could understand these people. They had such strange customs.

As the boys stood up and brushed the grass from their clothing, the Canadian visitors and Mrs. Edwards did a little play for their benefit. First, Mrs. Edwards faced the camera, and then she stood still. The man aimed it at her face and pushed a button. They heard a click and saw a sudden flash of light. Aram's heart stopped—it was like a trigger being pulled. But nothing happened. Mrs. Edwards was not hurt.

Then the man reached into an inner pocket in his suit jacket and pulled out an envelope. He motioned for the boys to crowd around. Inside the envelope were squares of cardboard with amazingly accurate black and white paintings of people. The man flipped through them all. He pulled one of them out and held it up to his face to show the boys. It was an image of him. Then he pointed at the camera and at the picture.

"Camera makes photographs."

He pointed to Aram. "You, *David Adams.*" And he gestured for Aram to step forward.

Aram didn't know what *David Adams* meant, but he looked into Mrs. Edwards' blue eyes. She nodded. Aram swallowed his fear and stepped forward. As he stood in front of the man, Aram stared at the round glass disc in the center of the wooden box. It was all he could do to keep from crying. In his mind, he saw his own father, standing helplessly as a soldier aimed a gun at his head.

Click! Flash!

Nothing.

Aram sighed in relief and stepped away.

In turn, each boy was called up to have his photograph taken. When Mrs. Edwards pointed at Mikayel, she said, "Michael Jones," and when she pointed to Zaven, she said, "Timothy Inkster."

Aram couldn't understand English, but he had an uneasy feeling that something wasn't right.

The boys spent the first week at the farm sleeping under the stars at night and running wild during the day. With just the reverend and Mrs. Edwards to supervise them, the boys had only two routines: meals and bedtime. Halfway through the week, a cook and a housekeeper arrived. But neither of them spoke Armenian.

Breakfast was always the dreaded porridge with skimmed milk and sugar. Lunch was sandwiches with the fluffy, tasteless Canadian bread. And supper was meat, vegetables, and potatoes—with stewed fruit for dessert. It took some of the boys several days to submit to the porridge. But once they realized that their stomachs would grumble until lunch if they didn't eat, they all eventually gave in.

Aram didn't care what it tasted like, as long as it was food. Having been hungry for so long, he felt as if he would never be rid of the hunger pangs. The other boys were the same. The Edwards were amazed at how much food the boys could eat. They didn't mind when the boys wrapped up any bits of uneaten food and took it back to their dormitory.

After supper on their seventh day, Reverend Edwards clapped his hands to get their attention. "Tonight you will all have your weekly shower," he said.

He gestured for them to follow. He led them into the long stucco building, down a set of stairs, and into a large, white tiled room. It was like nothing Aram had ever seen before. A series of strange metal pipes came out of the wall, way up high, and a row of handles was attached to the wall at about shoulder height.

"This is a shower," said Reverend Edwards.

"You turn on the tap," he said, pointing to a handle and then turning it. Suddenly, water sprinkled from the pipe above.

"You take off your clothing," said Reverend Edwards, pretending to take off his shirt and trousers.

Then, stepping under a shower head that wasn't turned on, he said, "And then you wash with soap."

He picked up a square white bar of soap and pretended to rub it all over himself.

Aram stifled a giggle. He looked over at Mikayel, who was chuckling, too. What did Reverend Edwards want? Should they take their clothing off and stand under the water? What did they need to do that for? There was a creek outside, and just this morning Aram had washed himself.

"Time for a shower," said Reverend Edwards, looking at each boy. "Timothy," he said, pointing to Zaven.

"Come here and have a shower."
Zaven shook his head and dashed out of the room.
The other boys followed.

Who is David?

D uring their second week at Georgetown, the mailman brought a big brown envelope.

"Boys, come here!" shouted Reverend Edwards, ringing a bell that could be heard throughout the farm.

Aram and Mikayel had been tossing a ball back and forth. Others had been wading in the creek, looking for fish. They all stopped what they were doing and ran to the reverend.

When Aram saw the envelope, his heart did a flip. Was this a package of letters from Corfu?

"Your photographs," said Reverend Edwards with a grin.

"Photographs?" Aram asked.

And then he remembered—the Canadians and the camera.

Reverend Edwards sat down at the picnic table and ripped open the envelope. The photos spilled out.

"Come," he motioned to the boys. They crowded round. The reverend fanned the photographs out on the table, so that they could all get a better look. Aram peered over Zaven's shoulder. What an odd sight it was, the solemn faces of all his friends in black and white.

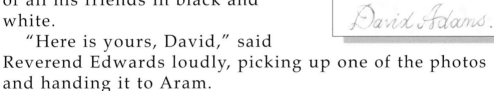

"Here is yours, David," said Reverend Edwards loudly, picking up one of the photos and handing it to Aram.

David? He shook his head in confusion. He remembered the day of the photographs and how none of the Canadians seemed to know the boys' names.

Aram stared into the sad dark eyes of the boy in the picture. *Is this what I look like?*

Something was written in English, in blue ink, along the bottom border of the photo. He could read Armenian but not English.

"What this say?" he asked Reverend Edwards.

"Your name," said the reverend. "David Adams."

Aram frowned in confusion. Very slowly, he said, "No. My name is Aram Davidian."

Reverend Edwards smiled but didn't reply. Instead, he sorted through the rest of the photos and began handing them out.

"Thomas Johnson," he said, looking at Taniel.

"Timothy Inkster," he said, looking at Zaven.

"Michael Jones," he said, looking at Mikayel.

After all of the photographs were handed out, Aram caught the angry look in Mikayel's eyes.

Aram nodded. "They've changed our names," he said.

On the first night that the boys were to sleep in their new bedroom, Mrs. Edwards held the door open. With their blankets thrown over their shoulders and their wooden traveling boxes clutched in front of them, they marched past her. Aram breathed in the scent of freshly waxed floors. On one side of the room was a row of bunk beds, similar to the ones they had slept on in the ship that brought them to Canada. On the other was a row of single beds. A pillow lay on each mattress.

Aram scrambled onto the top bunk of the bed closest to the door. "This one's mine," he said.

Taniel jumped onto the bottom bunk. "This one's mine," he shouted.

Aram peered over the side of the bunk. "I'm saving that one for Mgerdich."

"Oh!" said Taniel. He slid off that bed and scrambled up to the top bunk next to Aram's. "Good idea. I'll save my bottom bunk for Sarkis."

Mrs. Edwards brought in a stack of white cotton sheets and pillowcases. She clapped her hands.

"Boys, watch," she said. She demonstrated how to put a pillowcase on a pillow. Within moments of retrieving them, all of the boys had managed to slip their pillows inside pillowcases. Mrs. Edwards beamed.

"Now I will show you how to make a bed."

Aram paid attention as the reverend's wife tucked the corners of one of the white sheets around a mattress. When she was finished, the sheet was smooth and unwrinkled. Aram couldn't figure out how she did it. He tried it on his own mattress, but Mrs. Edwards came over to the side of his bed and shook her head.

"Like this," she said. She pulled here and there, and all at once his sheet was smooth. Mrs. Edwards went from bed to bed and tried to help. But with forty-six beds, and a room full of impatient and excited boys, it was no use.

She finally threw up her hands in frustration and left.

The boys were thrilled with their new bedroom. Aram pulled out a couple of slices of leftover bread from supper, and said, "Is anybody hungry?"

Mikayel grinned. He brought out a folded cloth from his own pocket and opened it up—a slice of beef. Another had found some wild berries in the bushes. The boys gathered round and, one by one, they all shared the bits of food they had hoarded. The boys chattered for hours and enjoyed their feast. But eventually they drifted off—all except Aram.

He punched his new pillow and tried to fall asleep. When he closed his eyes, he remembered his bed back home in Ulus. When his parents were alive, Aram, his mother, father, and his little brother would all cuddle together with pillows on the floor of the only room in their tiny home. In the center of the room was a *tonir*—a small, round metal plate. It covered a charcoal hearth that had been dug into the middle of their dirt floor, and it would keep their feet toasty warm on cool winter nights. Instead of a blanket they all snuggled under a large soft carpet. Aram's mother would tell them stories as they drifted off to sleep.

Aram tried to make sense of his new life. He could tell that Reverend Edwards and his wife wanted the best for every single boy in their charge. Aram was grateful for the food that they gave him. He was thankful to be in Canada, where he was safe. But at the same time, he felt empty and sad. He longed for a hug from his grand-mother, and he missed Mgerdich's grin. Here, there were no adults who could speak their language, and there was so much that Aram needed to find out.

He wanted to know about Mgerdich and whether he was still coming to Canada.

And what about Mr. Chechian? Their teacher, who had traveled with them to Canada and left for Ottawa to ask the government to make him a citizen. Aram wanted to know if Mr. Chechian was safe.

He wanted to know how he could send another letter to his grandmother.

And, most of all, he wanted to know why they kept calling him David.

"My name is Aram," he whispered under his breath.

CHAPTER 5

Mr. Alexanian

Aram had been kneeling at the side of the creek, skipping stones, when he heard an unfamiliar grumbling sound. It was followed by a strange honk. He looked up and saw billows of dust. A car came down the gravel laneway and stopped in front of the farmhouse.

Mrs. Edwards ran outside, drying her hands on her apron.

"Boys!" she called, "Come!"

As Aram approached, a tall man stepped out of the car. He was dressed like a Canadian, but his skin had a golden glow, and his eyes were the color of olives. He looked at the children who had gathered around him.

Then he said in Armenian, "So these are my boys."

Aram felt his heart swell with relief. This was the first time he had heard an adult speak Armenian since Mr. Chechian. Was this man staying with them? Did he speak English? Could he find out about how to mail letters? Could he find out about Mgerdich? The questions tumbled in his mind.

"Good day," said Aram in Armenian. He bowed deeply.

"And who do we have here?" asked the man in English, looking from Mrs. Edwards to Aram.

"This is David Adams," said Mrs. Edwards.

That name again, Aram thought to himself, but he kept silent. The Armenian man's smile dissolved into a faint frown.

"David Adams?" he said. "That is not an Armenian name."

"Call me Aram," said Aram, in slow and deliberate English. And then, in Armenian, he added, "My name is Aram Davidian."

"Ah," said the man. Also in Armenian, he answered, "Nice to meet you, Aram. My name is Mr. Alexanian."

The reverend's wife introduced Mr. Alexanian to the boys one by one, using their English names. As each stepped forward, they told the man what their Armenian names were.

After the introductions, Mr. Alexanian clapped his hands. "Come," he said in Armenian. "We have work to do."

He strode to the white stucco building, and the boys followed. When he got to their bedroom and saw the tangles of wrinkled sheets and blankets, he said, "In Canada, we make our beds."

Then he turned to Mrs. Edwards and said something to her in English. Her face lit up with a smile.

Mr. Alexanian snapped out orders.

"Each of you, take the blankets and sheets off your beds and shake out all the wrinkles. Now take one of the sheets and drape it over the bare mattress." And then he explained how to tuck in the sheets.

In no time, all forty-six beds were neatly made. Mrs. Edwards applauded. "Now, Mr. Alexanian," she said with a gleam in her eye. "Can you show these boys how to take their weekly shower?"

Dear Grandmother

Mr. Alexanian stayed for several days, and in that time he introduced the boys to a structured routine. Each morning they got up, made their beds, and marched down to the bathroom in the basement. They washed their hands and faces with soap and water, and they brushed their teeth.

He convinced the reverend and Mrs. Edwards to offer the boys something else for breakfast. So now, in addition to porridge, there was cornflakes. Aram thought that cornflakes was strange food, too; but he much preferred the golden crunchy flakes to the gray goo.

Mr. Alexanian divided the boys into five teams. "You are going to run this farm," he told them. The teams were assigned to cleaning, cooking, washing laundry, weeding, and raking.

"There will be cows and chickens coming soon," explained Mr. Alexanian,. "And you boys will be looking after them." He walked the boys through an empty barn and pointed out the newly built chicken coop.

It seemed like an adventure to Aram—the thought of running the farm themselves and having cows and chickens. "Pigs, too!" continued Mr. Alexanian, as he led the boys past a fenced-in area beyond the chicken coop.

The days flashed by, and Aram and the other boys settled in to the new routine. Everything was so much easier, now that Mr. Alexanian had arrived. But one day as Aram was sweeping the doorstep to the farmhouse, he saw Mr. Alexanian load his suitcase into the trunk of his car. Aram leaned his broom against the side of the house and ran over to the car.

"You're leaving us?" he asked.

"I will be back in a few days," said Mr. Alexanian.

"We thought you'd be living with us here," said Aram.

"I live in Toronto with my wife and children," said Mr. Alexanian. "When I found out that you boys had no translator, I came as fast as I could. But I can't stay."

Aram was crushed by the news. The arrival of Mr. Alexanian had cheered all of the boys. With him at the farm, living in Canada didn't feel nearly as strange.

"Couldn't your family come and live with us, too?" asked Aram.

Mr. Alexanian crouched so that he was eye level to Aram.

"I would love to do that," he said. "But I run a store in Toronto, and I can't be away for too long. Even now, my wife has to run the business alone."

Aram could feel the tears welling up in his eyes.

"Don't worry, Aram. I will be back. I have arranged for an Armenian couple to live at the farm with you."

"Thank you," said Aram.

"And there's something—," Aram began, but then he stopped. He was so choked with emotion that he couldn't speak.

"You're wondering about the boys who were held back in Paris?" asked Mr. Alexanian.

"Yes!" said Aram, surprised that the man knew so much.

"They'll be in Canada in a few days. I'll bring them to the farm myself."

"Oh!" said Aram. "Thank you." He hugged Mr. Alexanian with all his might.

Mr. Alexanian returned the hug. Then he held Aram at arm's length. He looked Aram in the eye again. "You're wondering about a sister or brother, too?"

"M...my grandmother," said Aram. "I mailed her a letter weeks ago, and I haven't got anything back."

"Don't be surprised if it takes another few weeks for you to get a letter," said Mr. Alexanian kindly. "It takes a long time for a letter to cross the ocean."

With that, he stood up and brushed the wrinkles out of his trousers. As Aram watched, Mr. Alexanian got into his car.

"Sir," said Aram urgently. "Would you mail a letter for me?"

"If you're speedy about it," answered Mr. Alexanian.

Aram ran back to the dorm and reached between his mattress and springs. He retrieved the photograph of himself that the Canadian had taken. Pulling out the wooden box from under his bed, he opened it up and found an envelope. It was already addressed to the orphanage in Corfu. He took a sheet of paper and scrawled in Armenian:

Dearest Grandmother,

This is a picture of what I look like now. I am fine. I am eating lots of food. I miss you, and I love you.

Aram.

He put the photo and the sheet in the envelope, and licked it shut.

He ran out of the dorm and over to the car. Mr. Alexanian was drumming his fingers on the steering wheel.

"I don't have a stamp, but I'll pay you back," said Aram.

"Don't worry," Mr. Alexanian said. "I'll use my own stamp. See you soon, son!" Then he drove away.

It wasn't until he was gone that Aram realized he hadn't asked about the English names.

CHAPTER 7

Wednesday, July 25, 1923:

A Surprise!

A week later, Aram was in the midst of the worst job at the farm—waxing the dining-room floor. He dipped his rag in the tin of wax and gingerly worked it into the gleaming wood in swirls.

"Ouch!" he pulled his hand away and looked closely at his index finger. A fine sliver of wood was jammed under his nail. He set down his rag and went to find Mrs. Edwards. She was in the kitchen, helping the cook put together a huge mound of sandwiches. When she saw Aram's finger, she set down her knife and went to the sewing kit.

She was poised over his finger with a hot sewing needle when Mikayel burst through the kitchen doorway.

"They're here!" he cried.

Mrs. Edwards used the momentary distraction to dig in with the needle and pry loose the sliver.

"Ow, ow, ow!" cried Aram.

"It's done," said Mrs. Edwards, dabbing his fingertip with iodine.

"Come on," said Mikayel from the doorway.

"Who's here?" asked Aram, waving his hand in the air to dry the iodine.

"The other boys, silly!" said Mikayel. Then he was gone. The door banged shut behind him.

Mgerdich is here! Aram forgot all about his sore finger. With a quick thanks to Mrs. Edwards, he ran outside. He saw that a cluster of boys had already gathered around the pathway that led to the train stop. The reverend and Mrs. Edwards hurried outside.

"It's Onnig and Hagop!" Aram could hear the boys calling.

"And Sarkis!"

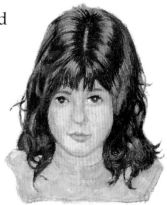

Aram reached the cluster of boys and elbowed his way through. Three boys stood in front of them.

Mgerdich wasn't there.

About ten steps behind Sarkis walked a little girl with scared eyes. She looked about a year younger than Mgerdich. A tall man and a young woman held the child's hands.

Aram gasped. The woman looked so much like his mother. Her black hair was caught at the nape of her neck in a loose bun, and she wore a homespun white blouse and the kind of long, black skirt that the missionaries in Corfu wore. Her face was etched with lines of worry.

A few steps behind the family was Mr. Alexanian. He held a stack of envelopes bound with twine. He had a big smile on his face, and when he spied Aram among the cluster of boys, he said, "See? I told you I would be back."

Mikayel ran to Sarkis. He grabbed him by the waist and tossed him in the air. "I'll show you all around," he said.

Sarkis grinned, dropped his box, and followed after the bigger boy. Others took Onnig and Hagop.

"Wait until you see this place," said Zaven excitedly.

Mr. Alexanian looked at Aram, and it was as if the man could read all of the confused thoughts that jumbled in the boy's head.

"The boys from Paris are here," said Mr. Alexanian. "I thought you'd be happy."

"I am," said Aram. "But one boy is still missing."

Mr. Alexanian frowned for a moment, and then his eyes lit up.

"You must mean Mgerdich."

"Yes," replied Aram.

"The cut to his face is taking a long time to heal," said Mr. Alexanian. "But don't worry. I am sure he will be sent to Canada soon."

But Aram was worried. He couldn't help it, thinking of poor Mgerdich, all alone in the Paris hospital.

"I have another question, too," said Aram, looking earnestly into Mr. Alexanian's face. "Have you heard anything about Mr. Chechian?"

Mr. Alexanian took a deep breath before he answered. "He is safe," he said.

Aram's heart skipped a beat. So the Canadian government decided to let him stay after all? This was wonderful news!

"Will he visit us?"

"He would love to, but he can't," replied Mr. Alexanian.

Aram frowned in confusion. "Why not?"

"The government isn't letting him stay," said Mr. Alexanian. "He is hiding."

"But—"

"No more questions, Aram. I need your help." Mr. Alexanian held out the package of envelopes.

"I know that you can read Armenian, but not all the

boys can. I would like you to sort through these letters and give them out."

Aram nodded. "I can do that," he said.

"Can you read the letters aloud for the younger boys?"

"Yes," said Aram.

He took the package from Mr. Alexanian's outstretched hand and hugged them to his chest. Would there be a letter from his grandmother? He dared not hope.

Mr. Alexanian ushered the Armenian couple over to the reverend and his wife. "I would like you to meet Kevork and Marta Adomian," he said. "And this is their daughter, Parantzim."

"Glad to meet you," said Reverend Edwards in a very loud voice.

"It is good to meet you, too," replied Kevork in perfect English.

Aram had planned to sort the letters on the picnic table, but the housekeeper had just placed a pyramid of sandwiches down. He went into the dormitory, but a bunch of boys were there, showing the new ones their bunks. Aram walked down the corridor to the dining room. His cloth and the tin of wax were still on the floor, so he put them away. Then he sat down by himself at the long dining room table.

He untied the knot on the bundle and spread the letters out. He knew which boys would be able to read their own letters, so he put those in one pile and the younger boys' letters into another. It wasn't until he got to the very bottom of the pile that he found a letter addressed to him. He tore it open hungrily and began to read the Armenian script:

> *Dear Aram,*
>
> *Your grandmother is standing beside me, telling me what to write. She says to give you all her love and to tell you that she is eating well and is happy that you are safe. I can vouch for the fact that she is eating well. I have hired her to work at the orphanage. She mends the clothing and peels the vegetables in exchange for food and a place to sleep. The children love her dearly. Please write when you are able to get paper and stamps.*
>
> *Your grandmother was thrilled to receive that long letter you wrote about your trip. Your letter and all the others arrived in one big package a few days ago. What an exciting trip you had! Your grandmother sends her love and so do I.*
> *Sincerely,*
> *Mrs. Walker.*
> *PS: Your grandmother says that she is proud of you.*

Aram held the letter to his chest and squeezed his eyes shut to keep from crying. It was such a relief to know that his grandmother was safe. And it was good to know that Mr. Chechian had been able to mail all of their letters.

The door burst open and the boys tumbled in. When they saw Aram sitting at the table with all the letters spread out in front of him, they ran over.

"Is there one for me?" asked Mikayel, anticipation in his voice.

"And me?" asked Zaven.

"And me?" asked Taniel.

The boys swarmed around the table and began to rifle through the letters. Two boys tugged on the same one and almost ripped it.

"Stop," said Aram, crouching over the letters protectively. "I'll call your names out one by one."

Soon all of the boys were lost in the words from home. Aram read the letters aloud for the younger boys.

It was a subdued group, and there was more than one sniffle.

Aram took his own letter and walked back to the bedroom. He tucked it in his wooden box for safekeeping, and then he went outside to find one of the new boys to ask for news of Mgerdich.

Sarkis looked at him and blinked. "I don't know," he answered. "He wasn't in the same part of the hospital where we were."

Aram kicked a twig hard with his toe. "You never saw him once?" he asked, disbelieving.

"No," said Sarkis. "It was a pretty big hospital!"

Aram turned on his heel and stomped off. He sat at the edge of the creek and skipped stones across it, trying to clear his mind. But he couldn't do it. He was relieved to know that Mr. Chechian was safe and he was glad that he had heard from his grandmother at last—that was such a worry off his mind. But Mgerdich! Aram had become his big brother. And Aram couldn't help his little brother at all.

"If this stone skips three times, then Mgerdich will be all right," said Aram. He angled the stone and threw it. The stone plopped and sank.

"Can I try?" said a soft voice in Armenian.

Startled, Aram looked up. It was Parantzim, the little girl.

"Sure," he said. "Let me find you a good stone."

"I found one already," she said, holding out a perfectly flat one in her thin hand. She bit her bottom lip, scrunched her face, and threw. The stone skipped three times.

"Mgerdich will be fine," she said.

Then she walked away.

Parantzim

O n the first night after the Adomians arrived, Aram thought about Parantzim. In some ways, he felt sorry for her. She shared a room with her parents on the second floor of the long stucco building. She didn't get to go to bed in a dormitory, whisper after lights out, and share secrets and bits of food like the boys did.

But he was also jealous. Watching her hold her mother's hand or sit on her father's lap had reminded him of how much he missed his parents. He took out the letter from his grandmother and tried to read it again. But the room was too dark. He fell asleep holding his letter to his heart.

Right after breakfast the next morning, Reverend Edwards rang his bell to gather everyone together. Beside him were a few large bowls and stacks of pails and wooden crates. He pointed to a distant part of the orchard and said something in English. Then he turned to Mr. Adomian to translate.

"Those are cherry trees," said Mr. Adomian, pointing in the same direction as the reverend had done. "Today we are going to pick cherries and fill these containers."

Aram's stomach grumbled with the thought of sweet, juicy cherries. They grew wild in Turkey, but he hadn't tasted one in years. He heard that cherries grew in Corfu, but he had never seen any. It wasn't surprising—after all, every tree and plant had been picked clean by the thousands of Armenian orphans who had taken refuge there.

Aram raised his hand.

"Yes?" said Mr. Adomian.

"Please, sir. May we eat the cherries while we pick?"

Mr. Adomian grinned. "Yes, you may. The reverend says you may eat your fill while you're picking."

At this news, the boys cheered and scrambled to get the biggest containers they could manage.

"One more thing," said Mr. Adomian. "You will be paid for what you bring back to him."

Containers in hand, the boys raced to the cherry orchard. Mrs. Adomian and her daughter also came, but

Mr. Adomian and Reverend Edwards stayed behind.

Once the boys got to the orchard, they ran to the nearest cherry trees and reached up for the luscious red fruit on the lowest branches. They picked by the handful, filling their mouths as efficiently as they filled their pails, bowls, and crates. They spit their pits onto the ground like bullets.

Aram climbed one of the trees, and Mikayel stood below him, pail outstretched. Balancing his feet on a sturdy branch, Aram was able to reach clusters of cherries hidden deep within the greenery. In no time, he and Mikayel had filled a whole pail. They ran to another tree, and this time it was Mikayel's turn to scramble up. Once their wooden crate was full, Mikayel stuffed his shirt with cherries and then his pockets.

"Here," he called down to Aram. "Open your shirt."

He threw bunches of cherries down and Aram stuffed so many in his shirt until not another single cherry would fit. Mikayel jumped down, and then the two boys sat against a tree and ate to their heart's content. The cherries were as sweet and delicious as the butterscotch candy. And the best part was that they could have more than one.

Aram looked around and saw that most of the other boys had filled their single containers, and that their mouths bulged with cherries. Aram was thankful he wasn't on laundry duty this week. Only two people were still picking cherries—Mrs. Adomian and Parantzim. Aram counted their containers. The Adomians had already filled three pails and one wooden crate between them. Parantzim's lips were unstained by cherry juice.

"Aren't you going to eat any?" he asked her.

"Maybe later," she said. "But I want to pick as many as I can."

"Why?" he asked.

"I want to earn lots of money," she said. 'If we give it to the reverend, maybe he can bring over more orphans."

Suddenly Aram's stomach felt like it was about to burst. Why hadn't he thought of that? He could save his money and send it to his grandmother. And if they all put some of their money together, then maybe they could save some more orphans, too.

"Boys!" he shouted, "Let's get more containers!"

CHAPTER 9

Learning English

Parantzim shied away from most of the boys, but she felt comfortable around Aram. They would often skip stones together at the creek, or watch for frogs and tiny fish.

The boys adored Mrs. Adomian. Each night as they were drifting off to sleep, she would come in and sing an Armenian lullaby. Sometimes, in the dark, she would tell them an Armenian folk tale. The boys called her *Mairig*, which means *Mother*.

If one of them had a sliver or a scraped knee, they came to Mrs. Adomian now, and she kissed it better. Mrs. Edwards didn't seem to mind. She would look on and smile, happy that this Armenian mother could bring a bit of home into the lives of the orphaned boys.

Now that the Adomians could translate, the boys started daily classes. Between school and the work chores, the boys had long and productive days. Each morning, the reverend would teach the boys English grammar and vocabulary, and then Mrs. Edwards would teach them songs and hymns in English. Soon Aram found that he was able to say a sentence or two at a time in English. As long as he spoke slowly, the reverend and his wife would nod in understanding. Mikayel also progressed rapidly in English, although it came more slowly to most of the boys.

The best part of the school day was the late afternoon, when Mrs. Adomian would read them a story in Armenian. At the very end of the day, Mr. Adomian would teach them Armenian history.

One day in Mr. Adomian's class, Aram put up his hand.

"Please, sir. Why do the Canadians call us by the wrong names?"

Mr. Adomian's eyes clouded over with the question. "It cost a lot of money to bring you here," he said.

"Yes," said Aram. The other boys nodded. "We are grateful to the Canadians for bringing us."

"They think it would be easier for you to adjust to your new life if you have Canadian names. So each of you has been given the name of a benefactor."

The boys looked stunned.

Aram's lower lip quivered. "I...I guess we should be honored to have their names."

Mr. Adomian opened his mouth then shut it again, pressing his lips tight. After a moment, he said, "Let us continue with our lesson."

Sunday August 12, 1923

One More Visitor

It was Sunday morning, so the boys dressed in their cleanest clothing. They put on their new shoes and socks and marched into town. Since there were no Armenian churches in Georgetown, they would go to a different church each Sunday. Today it was the United Church. As always, the boys were asked to sing a hymn. The church was packed with more than just United Church parishioners. It thrilled Aram that the Canadians seemed to love to hear them sing.

In the afternoon, some people came to visit the farm, and one of the ladies gave Aram three pennies. He put two of the pennies in the wooden box under his bed.

This is for you, Grandmother, he said to himself. And this is for our orphan, he thought as he dropped the third penny into a glass jar on the mantle in the dormitory. The boys had started up a collection with some of their cherry-picking money. The jar was already halfway full.

After the Canadians left, Aram sat alone, leaning against a willow tree by the creek. He was almost happy. He had plenty of food, and he was safe and surrounded by friends. He loved the Georgetown farm, and he was beginning to feel almost Canadian. Being so far away from his grandmother was hard. But her letter had warmed his heart, and he knew that Mrs. Walker was taking care of her. But something else was still missing.

He heard a car approaching. At first he thought it was more Canadians, but then, as the car got closer, he recognized it as Mr. Alexanian's. Maybe he was bringing Mgerdich? Aram dared not hope. He had been disappointed too many times. Probably he was bringing more letters.

Aram took a deep breath and walked up to the car as it pulled to a stop. Mr. Alexanian stepped out of the driver's seat...and then the passenger door opened. Aram saw two sandaled feet emerge, and then he saw a shock of black hair. The door slammed shut.

There stood Mgerdich!

He was even thinner than he had been in Corfu, and he also seemed shorter—but Aram knew that he was the one

who had grown chubbier and taller. Along Mgerdich's left cheek was a long red scar with stitch marks. It looked like a railway track.

"It is so good to see you," said Aram, suddenly shy.

Aram felt like clasping Mgerdich in his arms and throwing him in the air, but the little boy looked fragile, and even a bit frightened. His eyes were round like saucers as he took in the farm, the buildings, and his suddenly large friend.

"Come on," said Aram, gesturing with his hand. "I'll show you around."

The boys were delighted to see that Mgerdich had finally arrived. They took turns showing him the pigs, the cows, the chickens, the schoolroom, and their dormitory. Mrs. Edwards and the cook made a platter of sandwiches and brought out flags—so that he would have the same welcome as the other boys. Mr. and Mrs. Adomian and Parantzim stood grinning in welcome, and all the boys cheered, singing, "For He's a Jolly Good Fellow."

Reverend Edwards held out his hand in greeting. "I am glad to meet you, John MacDonald," he said.

Mgerdich frowned in confusion. He searched the eyes of the forty-nine boys who were crowded around him, but none of them explained to him what Reverend Edwards meant.

Mr. Adomian cleared his throat and said, "Mgerdich, the reverend is greeting you with your new Canadian name."

Mgerdich looked startled.

"But...I...," he said. Then he stopped. He shook the reverend's hand and bowed deeply.

"My name is Mgerdich Safarian," he said in Armenian. Reverend Edwards, not understanding, simply nodded.

That night after the lights were out, the dormitory buzzed with questions.

"Why did they keep you at the hospital so long?"

"Did you have your own room?"

"Did anyone speak Armenian at the hospital?"

Mgerdich would barely have time to answer one question when the next would tumble on top of the first.

"Enough," he said finally. "I have my own questions."

The room fell silent.

"What is this about my name?"

"They've changed all of our names," said Zaven. "I am Timothy Inkster, and that boy," he said, pointing at Aram, "is David Adams."

Aram grinned, as if it was all a joke, but inside he felt like crying.

"My name is Aram," he said. "Not David."

"I am not going to change my name," said Mgerdich firmly.

"I don't want to change mine either," said Aram. "But these Canadians who saved our lives have given us their own names. How can we tell them that we don't want those names without hurting their feelings?"

"There has to be a way," said Mgerdich.

A Full Fifty

Threw boys got up early the next morning. They
washed and dressed. Then Aram told Mr. and Mrs.
Adomian of their plan.

"I will translate for you," said Mr. Adomian.

All fifty boys marched to the farmhouse with
Parantzim and Mr. and Mrs. Adomian at their side. Aram
took in one deep breath for courage and knocked on the
door. Mrs. Edwards answered.

"What's this?" she asked, when she saw how serious
they looked.

"The boys would like to have a meeting with you and

Reverend Edwards," explained Mr. Adomian. "They have asked me to translate."

Mikayel shuffled up to the front, his eyes downcast.

"Please, sir." he said carefully in English. "Call me Mikayel Assadourian, not Michael Jones. I don't feel like a Michael Jones."

Zaven stepped forward. He looked first at Mrs. Edwards, and then at the reverend. "Thank you for saving my life," he said. "Please call me Zaven Manougian, not Timothy Inkster."

Then he wiped away a tear with the back of his hand and said, "Manougian may be hard for you to say, but Inkster is hard for me. This name has been in my family for a thousand years. It is older than Canada."

Then Taniel stepped forward.

"My name is not Thomas Johnson. My name is Taniel Papazian."

He took a deep breath and continued. "My sister is still in Corfu. Her name is Papazian, too. How will she find me if my name is Johnson?"

"Boys," said Reverend Edwards. "We thought that we were helping you by giving you good Canadian names—names that are easy to pronounce. Don't you want to forget about your sadness and hunger in the past? Don't you want to start a new life in Canada?"

"Thank you for our new life," said Aram. "We are glad

to be Canadian, but we don't want to forget where we came from."

Aram pointed at Mgerdich. "See that little boy?" he asked. "When he was a baby, an Armenian priest poured water on his head and named him Safarian, after his father and mother. Now he has lost his father and mother. He has lost his homeland, too. All that he has left is his name. Please don't take that away from him. Call him Mgerdich, please."

Reverend Edwards was so overcome with emotion that he couldn't say a word. Mrs. Edwards dabbed her eyes with a handkerchief.

"Children," she said. "We will make this right."

At bedtime that night, Aram, Mgerdich, Taniel, Mikayel, Zaven, and all of the other boys brought out of their pockets the bits of food they had gathered over the course of the day.

"It's time to celebrate," said Aram, as he put his bread crusts on Mgerdich's mattress. "Let's have a party!"

Aram and Taniel and Mikayel and Zaven and all the others shared their food and celebrated the arrival of Mgerdich. And they celebrated the return of their own names.

Aram declared, "My name is Aram Davidian.
And I am a Canadian."
He would never get tired
of saying that.

above: Boys in the orchard at the farm

below: Boys in the pasture, 1926

above: Digging a drainage ditch

above: The first fifty, 1924

opposite top left: The real Mr. Aris Alexanian
opposite top right: The farmhouse today
opposite bottom left: Onnig and Markar Shangayan: brothers reunited in 1924
opposite bottom middle: Near East relief poster produced in 1918
opposite bottom right: In the fields at the farm, 1925

YOUR BIT SAVES A LIFE

2½ Million Women and Children
Now Starving to Death

You Can't Let Us Starve

Armenian and Syrian Relief Campaign
508 Wm. Penn Place (Union Arcade)
PITTSBURGH, PA.

BY THE SPRING OF 1923, 4,000 Armenian children had taken refuge on the Greek island of Corfu. They had escaped Turkey, where 1.5 million Armenians had been killed during the first genocide of the twentieth century. Most of the children who were living in Corfu were now orphans.

The Armenian Relief Association of Canada was formed in 1922 with the goal of rescuing 100 orphaned boys between the ages of eight and twelve and setting them up on a farm in Southern Ontario. There the young refugees would be cared for, educated, and trained as farm helpers. The first of the Armenian refugees, who became known as the Georgetown Boys, arrived in Georgetown, Ontario, on July 1, 1923.

On their first night, the boys did indeed sleep under the stars. They were delighted with flushing toilets and real showers. And although they really did hate porridge, the boys were overwhelmed by the wide variety and quantity of food they were offered. Visitors came from all around to see the children, who were quite a novelty; their rescue was Canada's first international relief effort.

The character of Mr. Alexanian is based on the real Mr. Aris Alexanian, who founded Alexanian Carpets in Hamilton, Ontario, in 1925. He interpreted for the boys when they first arrived. The Alexanian family kindly supplied Muriel Wood with family photographs so that Mr. Alexanian's likeness in the book could be accurate.

The Georgetown boys were actually assigned new names. But they demanded to keep their own names, and they succeeded; the scene that depicts this incident is accurate and almost word-for-word.

After fifty years in Canada, the original Georgetown Boys recorded interviews on tape about their escape from Turkey, their time in Corfu, their journey to Canada, and their first few years in Canada. The tapes are held by the Multicultural History Society of Ontario in Toronto.

Marsha Skrypuch became interested in the Georgetown Boys in the late 1980s. She listened to the interview tapes and took notes, but she soon discovered that she could not complete her research for *Aram's Choice* and *Call Me Aram*. The most complete interviews had been sealed and would not be made available until after all the Georgetown Boys had passed away. These interviews contained graphic and detailed eyewitness accounts of the Armenian Genocide, an event that the Turkish government denies to this day. As eyewitnesses, the boys feared for their safety. In 2003, after the last Georgetown Boy had died, the final tapes were unsealed. Marsha Skrypuch was able to complete her research. The boys are gone, but their words live on.

Ankara—A province in present-day Turkey, an area where Armenians have lived for centuries.

Armenians—An ancient people who populated a vast region in Asia Minor, including present-day Turkey. It is said that they can trace their ancestry back to Noah, and Mount Ararat, believed to be the last resting place of the Ark after the Great Flood, is in ancient Armenia. The Armenians adopted Christianity in 301 AD, making them the first state to do so. Armenians and Turks have been uneasy neighbors for five centuries, with various Turkish kingdoms conquering Armenia over time. The Armenians' quest for autonomy in their own homeland was considered treason by various Turkish governments.

Corfu—An island in Greece. Many Armenians, who fled Turkey in 1923, took refuge in Greece.

Dormitory—A large room or building used as a sleeping chamber for large numbers of people.

Icebox—Before refrigerators became common in homes around 1930, people put blocks of ice into an insulated cabinet, called an icebox, where they kept their food cold.

Iodine—A mixture of 10% iodine with ethanol is used to disinfect wounds.

Lahvosh—Flat, crispy bread made without yeast.

Mairig—Armenian for Mother.

Missionary—A person who goes to another country to give aid. Originally, missionaries were sent to non-Christian countries to convert the people to Christianity.

Ojak—Cooking hearth

Orchard—An area of land planted with fruit trees.

Orphanage—A home for large groups of children whose parents have died.

GLOSSARY

Pilaf—Cracked wheat cooked in broth

Porridge—Oatmeal boiled in water

Radial railway—Decades ago, people could travel from city to city in Ontario by electric railway. A huge network of radial railways in Southwestern Ontario connected Toronto, Hamilton, London, Guelph, and even smaller cities and towns. This form of transportation was abandoned when cars became popular.

Reverend—A title for a member of the Christian clergy.

Stucco—A mixture of cement, sand, and lime that is used on the outside of buildings to insulate them.

Tonir—A small charcoal hearth dug into the middle of the floor in a traditional Armenian home. It is covered with a metal plate and is used to warm nuts and fruit. A family sleeps around the tonir, their feet facing the hearth to keep their toes

toasty warm. Families also gather around the tonir for storytelling.

Turkey—A country situated between Western Asia and Southeastern Europe. The original Turks were clusters of nomadic tribes who came to the region of modern day Turkey in 800 AD. The Turkish nation adopted the Muslim religion centuries ago. Armenian and Turkish cultures lived side by side for centuries, intermarrying and trading together but keeping their own distinct cultures. Because of their long and close contact, there is no racial difference between Turks and Armenians. The difference is cultural and religious. Modern Turkey is the only middle/near eastern country that is secular—ruled by a non-religious government.

Ulus—A village in Ankara, Turkey

United Church—A Christian denomination. Armenians are also Christian.

Suggested Reading

For Young Readers

Skrypuch, Marsha Forchuk.
Aram's Choice. Markham: Fitzhenry &
Whiteside, 2006.

For Older Readers

Apramian, Jack. *The Georgetown Boys*.
Revised, edited with an introduction
by Lorne Shirinian. Toronto:
Zoryan Institute, 2008.
For purchasing information, please
contact: zoryan@zoryaninstitute.org
or phone 416-250-9807

Kherdian, David. *The Road from Home*.
New York: Greenwillow, 1995.

Marshall, Bonnie C., Translator,
*The Flower of Paradise and
Other Armenian Tales*: Westport:
Libraries Unlimited, 2007.

Shirinian, Lorne. *The Landscape of

*Memory: Perspectives on the Armenian
Diaspora*. Kingston:
Blue Heron Press, 2006.

Skrypuch, Marsha Forchuk.
Daughter of War. Markham:
Fitzhenry & Whiteside, 2008.

Skrypuch, Marsha Forchuk.
The Hunger. Toronto:
Dundurn Press, 1999.

Skrypuch, Marsha Forchuk.
Nobody's Child. Toronto:
Dundurn Press, 2004.

SUGGESTED READING

INTERNET

Armenian National Institute:
http://www.armenian-genocide.org/

The author's website:
http://www.calla.com

FILM

The Georgetown Boys
Producer/Director: Dorothy
Manoukian
Canadian Filmmakers Distribution
Centre, 1987.
DVD (26 minutes).
For purchasing information, please
contact: gtb@photographos.com
or phone 514-338-3862.

The Georgetown Boys
by Isabel Kaprielian
DVD (12 minutes)
Includes teacher's guide

For purchasing information, please
contact: isabelk@csufresno.edu
or phone: (416) 769-0843

My Son Shall Be Armenian
Director/Researcher: Hagop
Goudsouzian
National Film Board of Canada, 2005.
VHS (81 minutes)
With subtitles: available in original
French version: *Mon Fils Sera
Arménien.*
For purchasing information, please
contact: www.nfb.ca
or phone 514-283-9450

I N D E X

I N D E X

M

Mairig, 60

meals, 24
    see also food

Mgerdich, 10, 17, 18, 45, 52, 53
    return of, 65, 68

Mikayel, 7, 8, 13, 22, 47, 56

Minnedosa, 16

missionary, 8, 46

money, 57, 63, 64

mother, 16, 17, 32, 33

N

names, new, 22, 29, 30, 33, 36, 43, 74
    problems with, 66, 68
    reason for, 61, 62
    solution to, 70, 71

O

oatmeal porridge, 11, 13, 24, 74

ojak, 17

orchard, 55

orphanage, 7, 9, 16, 17, 50

P

Parantzim, 53, 54, 57

photographs, 22, 28, 29, 42

pilaf, wheat-berry, 17

porridge, oatmeal, 11, 13, 24, 74

R

radial railway, 17

Reverend Edwards, 10
    see also Edwards, Reverend

routine, 38, 39

S

Sarkis, 47, 52

school, 61

shower, 25, 27

sliver, 44, 45

stove, 16, 17

stucco, 10, 25, 37, 54

supper, 24

T

tonir, 32, 33

Turkey, 7, 9, 55, 74, 75

U

Ulus, Turkey, 16, 17, 32

United Church, 63

W

wheat-berry pilaf, 17

Z

Zaven, 11, 13, 22, 26, 27

B I O G R A P H Y

MARSHA FORCHUK SKRYPUCH is the author of many books for children, including *Daughter of War, Prisoners in the Promised Land, Nobody's Child, Silver Threads, Enough, The Hunger, and Hope's War. Aram's Choice* was nominated for the Silver Birch Express Award, the CLA Children's Book of the Year Award, and the Golden Oak Award; it was also listed by *Resource Links* as a *Best Book*. Sam Hancock adapted the *Aram* books into a play called *The Georgetown Boys*; and in May, 2008, the Georgetown Little Theatre performed it to sold-out crowds. Also in May, 2008, in recognition for her outstanding achievements in the development of the culture of Ukraine, Marsha was awarded the Order of Princess Olha by Victor Yushchenko, President of Ukraine. An English scholar and former librarian, Marsha lives with her husband in Brantford, Ontario.

BIOGRAPHY

MURIEL WOOD was born in Kent, England. She obtained her diploma in design and painting at the Canterbury College of Art before immigrating to Canada. Since the early 1960s, her artwork has appeared in many places: magazines, books, stamps, porcelains, and posters. In addition, she has displayed her paintings in a number of group and one-woman shows. Her children's books include *Old Bird*, L.M. Montgomery's *Anne of Green Gables*, and Margaret Laurence's *The Olden Day's Coat*. She has also illustrated the three previous titles in the *New Beginnings* series: *Aram's Choice, Scared Sarah*, and *Lizzie's Storm*. A former instructor at the Ontario College of Art and Design in Toronto, Muriel now draws and paints full-time. She lives with her husband in Toronto, Ontario.

Boys in the orchard at the farm (p.74) Courtesy of Archives Canada. Immigration Branch / Library and Archives Canada / PA-147571

Boys in the pasture, 1926 (p. 75) Courtesy of the Multicultural History Society of Ontario

Digging a drainage ditch (p. 75) Courtesy of the Multicultural History Society of Ontario

The first fifty, 1924 (p.76) Source unknown, Courtesy of the Multicultural History Society of Ontario

The real Mr. Aris Alexanian (p.77) Courtesy of Aris Alexanian

The farmhouse today (p.77) Courtesy of Muriel Wood

Brothers reunited (p. 77) John and his little brother, United Church of Canada Archives, Board of Evangelism and Social Service Fonds, [ca. 1927]

Near East Relief poster (p.77) "Your Bit Saves a Life" Courtesy of the Zoryan Institute.

In the fields at the farm, 1925 (p.77) Courtesy of Archives Canada. Immigration Branch / Library and Archives Canada / PA-148138